WHOOP!

An Aggie
Football Weekend

Written By: CINDY KING BOETTCHER

Illustrated By: TAMMIE L. BISSETT

To my husband Ben
and daughters, Rachel and Amy -
And the wonderful memories
of our first Football Weekends at Texas A&M!
Love, C.K.B.

A special thanks to our neighbors,
Ryan '87 & Nancy (New) '88 Jahns,
and their precious Aggie children -
Jill, Ty, and Meg.
Thanks, "My Boettchers".

In memory of my dad, Wallace S. Phillips, Jr. '71.
His extraordinary grace, courage, and strength
during his last year of life give me inspiration
as I journey through mine.
I love you Dad. T.L.B.

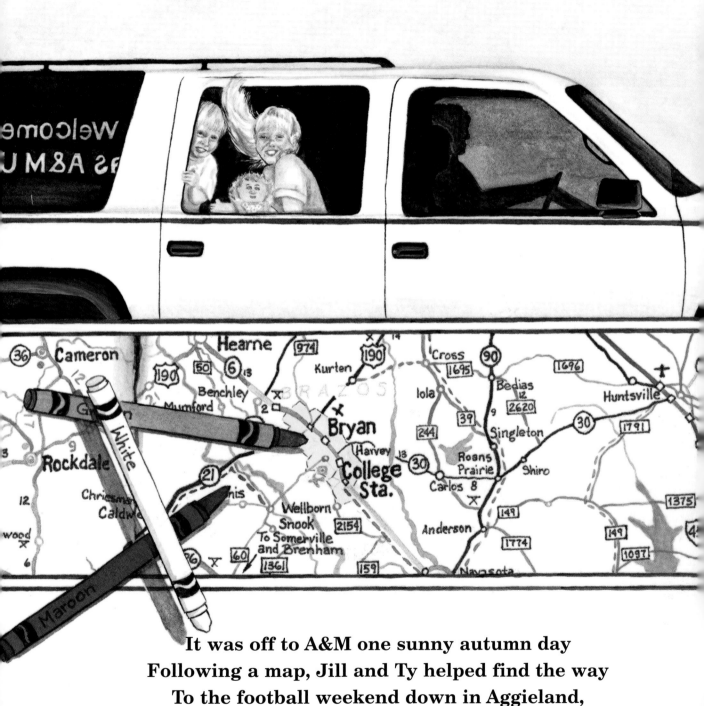

It was off to A&M one sunny autumn day
Following a map, Jill and Ty helped find the way
To the football weekend down in Aggieland,
Part of the Tradition of this school so grand.

Their first stop was at a campus bookstore
To buy new clothes to watch the Aggies score.
Decked out in their outfits of maroon and white
They certainly looked a handsome sight!

At the hotel, they would spend the night.
Mom and Dad had warned, "No pillow fights!"
While swimming and splashing water on the tiles
Their laughter echoed for several miles.

As the sky grew dark and the time got late,
They arrived on campus through Northgate.
A Drum Major helped them join in with the Band,
Then they swayed to *The War Hymn* in Aggieland.

They marched to Kyle Field for Midnight Yell
Observing the Yell Leaders so they could tell,
When to do "Aggies" or "Farmers Fight"
Capturing the spirit that makes Aggies unite!

On Saturday morning while the sun did shine
Jill and Ty arrived at the Quad to find –
Miss Reveille, favorite puppy, Mascot of A&M,
While they hugged her, Mom took their picture again.

Showing
them the statue of
the famous Twelfth Man,
Dad explained to the twins why
Aggies must stand –
Always ready to assist their team
through a game,
The two were now ready to do the same.

They approached Kyle Field with a program in their hands
And heard the brassy sounds of the Texas Aggie Band.
With hot dogs, drinks, and assorted snacks for the stands,
They headed to their seats with the other Aggie fans.

Keeping a steady beat, Corps Outfits marched in
With military precision from beginning to end.
To keep them in step as they marched around
The Band played loudly in the background.

"Whoop!" the fans yelled as players entered Kyle Field,
Reveille barking loudly by her Mascot Keeper's heel.
The players paused with their helmets in hand,
While fans proudly sang *The Spirit of Aggieland*.

The kickoff took place, Aggies made their first down –
A pass from the quarterback - the receiver was found.
He ran to the goal line - six points, a touchdown,
Then Ty kissed Jill - It's Tradition in this town!

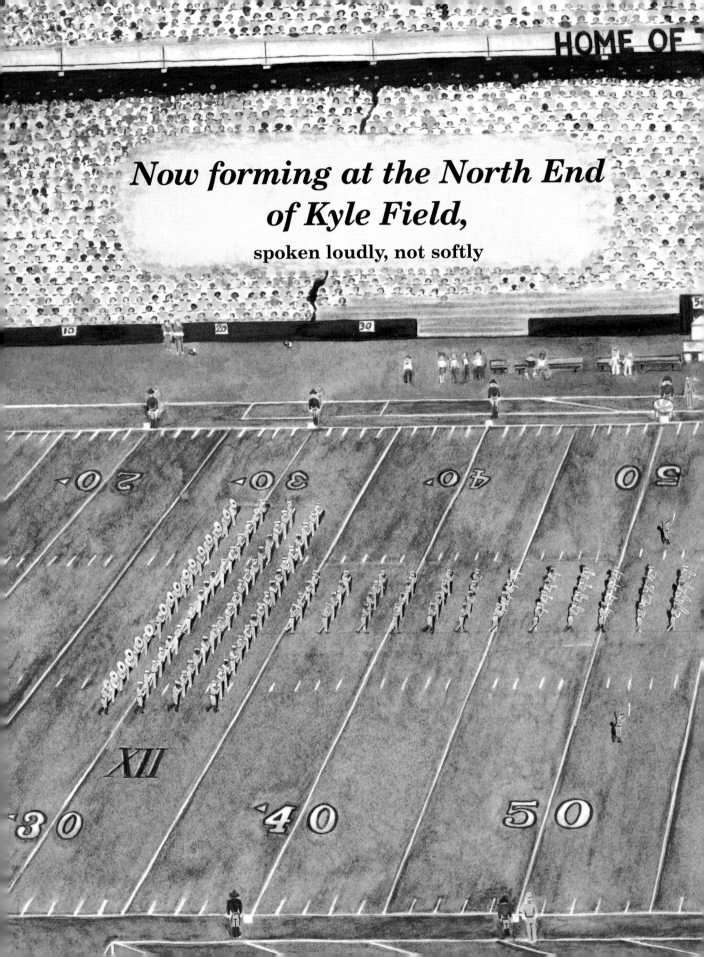

Silver bugles flashed as Senior Cadets stepped off.
Three drum majors led the band through intricate drills,
The famous "Block T" gave the crowd such a thrill.

Second half started, and our opponents scored.
All of a sudden, we could hear the Ags roar,
"Riffity, riffity, riff, raff," the fans were most upset
At the referees' call, it had not been their best.

Suddenly behind as the game neared the end
The Wrecking Crew arrived - their team's victory to defend.
An interception, followed by the winning touchdown
Created much wildcatting in this famous Aggie Town.

Fish gathered on the field for their frenzied chase
To catch Yell Leaders who scrambled in haste.
Despite their efforts, into "Fish Pond" they did dive
And fans for a victory Yell Practice arrived.

Later, Jill and Ty strolled back to their car
To enjoy a tailgate party with friends from afar.
They laughed and played till the sun went down
Then tiredly travelled to their own hometown.

As the twins rode home from College Station that night,
They looked back at A&M - to remember the sights
Of the places and friends they had seen that day,
At Kyle Field where the Fightin' Texas Aggies play.

It was their first football weekend at Aggieland,
"But it won't be the last," said Mom and Dad.
They talked of the games in the years to come
Holding tight to the memories of the day just done.

Printed by Quebecor Printing-Kingsport.
Typography by Charlie Kelm, Newman Printing Company.
Separations and prepress by Characters, Houston, Texas.

Library of Congress Cataloging-in-Publication Data
Boettcher, Cindy King
Whoop! / Cindy King Boettcher. p. cm.
Summary: Young Aggie Twins experience
their first football weekend at Texas A&M University.
ISBN 0-9652751-1-6
[1. Picture Book   2. College - Fiction   3. Stories in Rhyme]
1997
First Printing, July 1997

Cindy King Boettcher '76 has been a teacher and school principal for twenty years. She is an avid collector of children's literature and is currently completing her doctoral studies in the College of Education at Texas A&M University, where she has taught children's literature and supervised student teachers. *Whoop!* is her third book. She is also the author of *Anna Meagan, The Aggie Cinderella Story*, and co-author of *Breaking the Circle of One: Redefining Mentorship in the Lives and Writings of Teacher Educators.*

Her husband Ben, Class of '72, is an architect, and they live in Brenham, Texas, with their two daughters. For additional copies of this book and other publications, Cindy can be reached toll free at 1-800-233-5891, or on her home page http://www.phoenix.net/~cindyb

Tammie L. Bissett is best known for bringing a smile to Aggies all over the world with paintings and prints such as "Anticipation", "The Saturday Evening Aggies", and "Changing of the Guard". She has been a professional artist for over fifteen years and has been painting artwork depicting Texas A&M University for the past four years. Her husband Wesley, received his DVM Degree from the College of Veterinary Medicine in 1997. They reside in Dripping Springs, Texas, with their three children. For additional information concerning Tammie's art work, she can be reached toll free at 1-888-826-3947.